Noisy Traffic

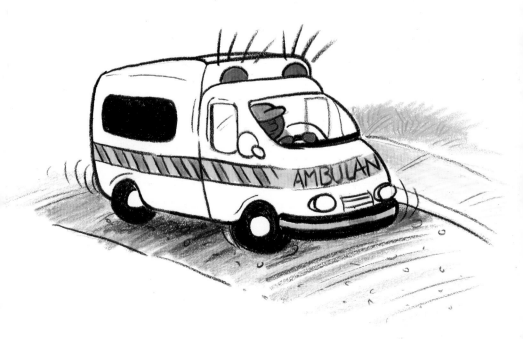

written by Pam Holden
illustrated by Pauline Whimp

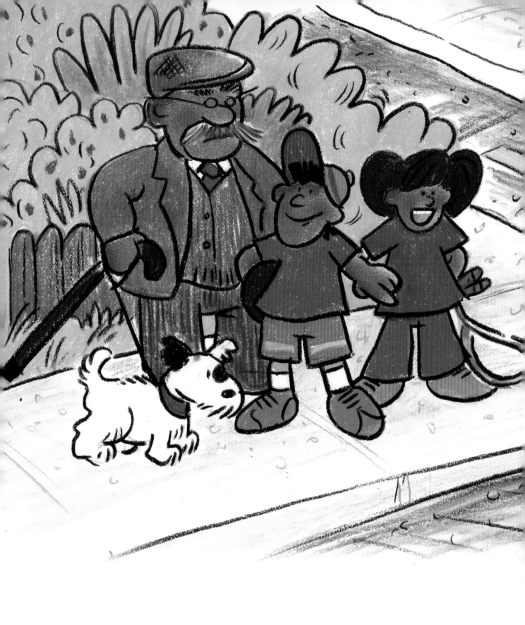

C is for car.

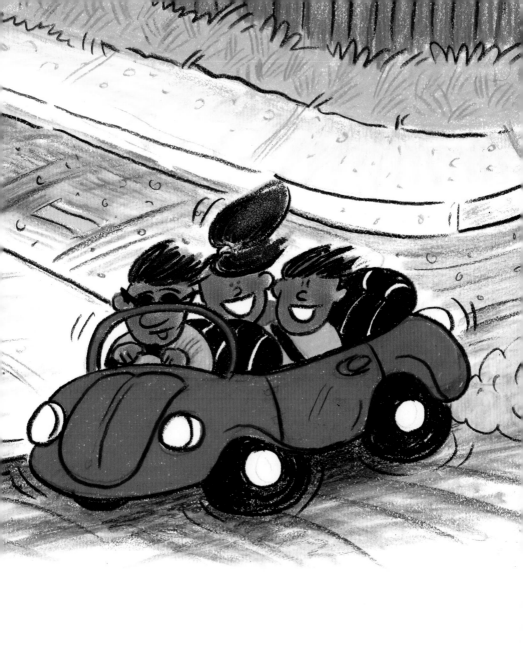

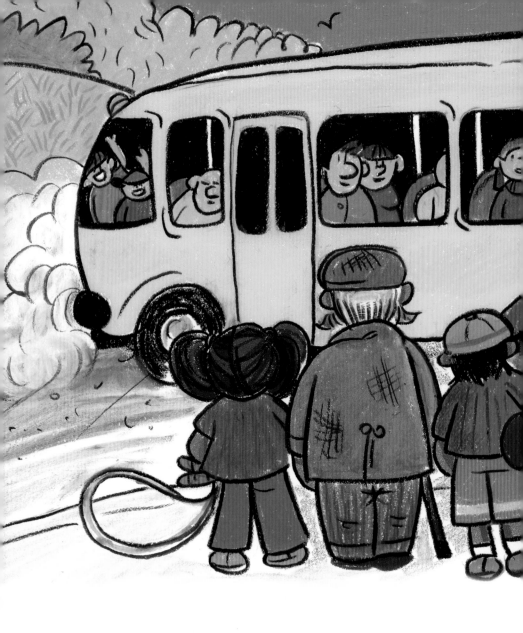

B is for bus.

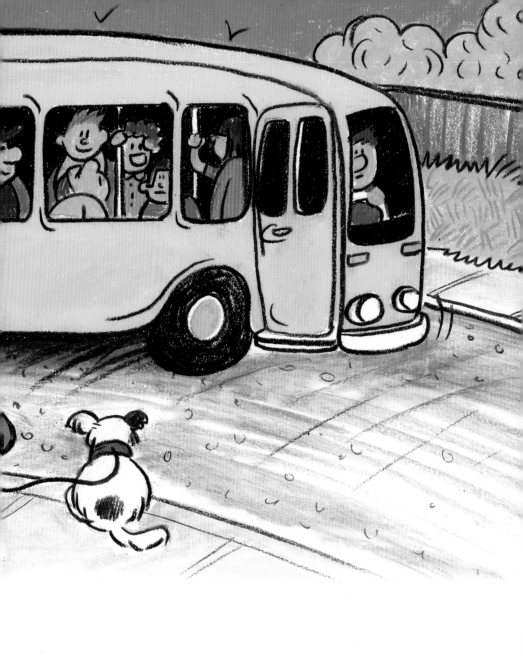

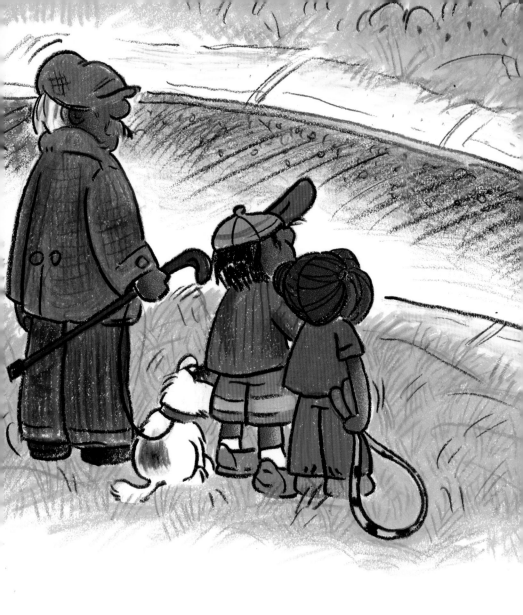

T is for truck.

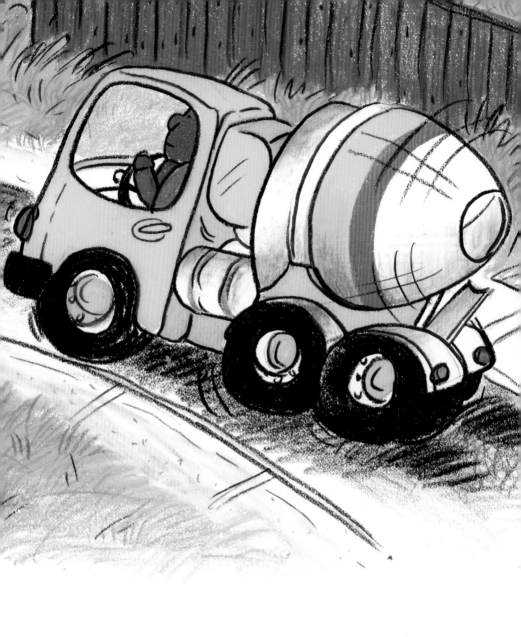

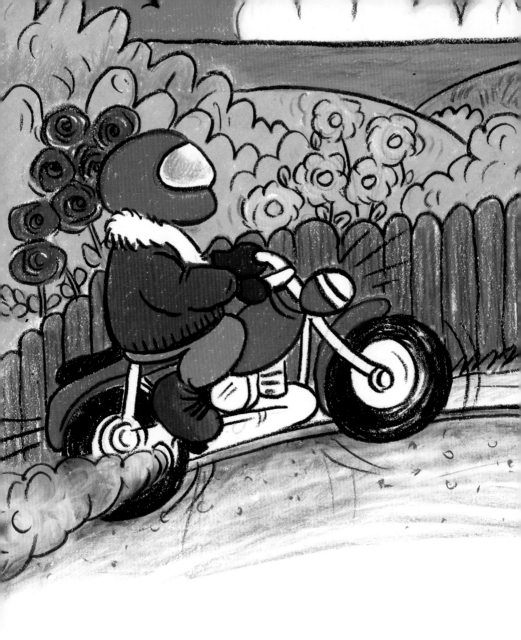

M is for motorcycle.

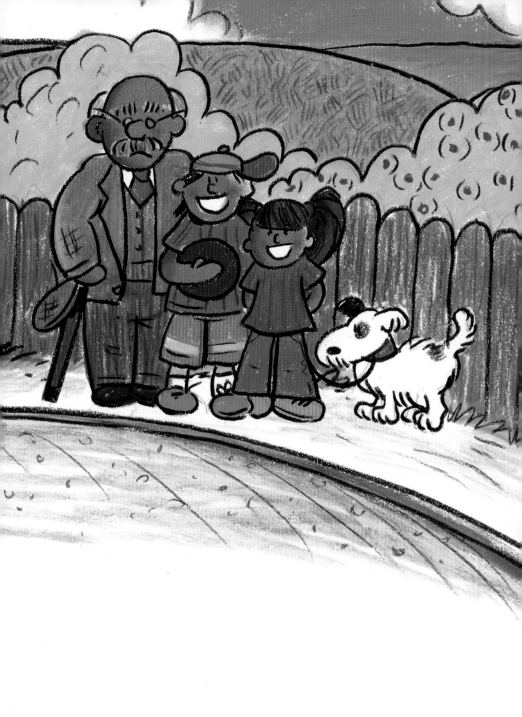

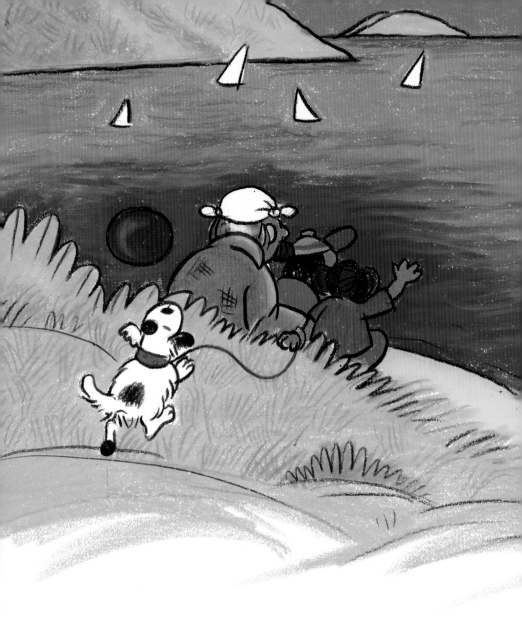

B is for boat.

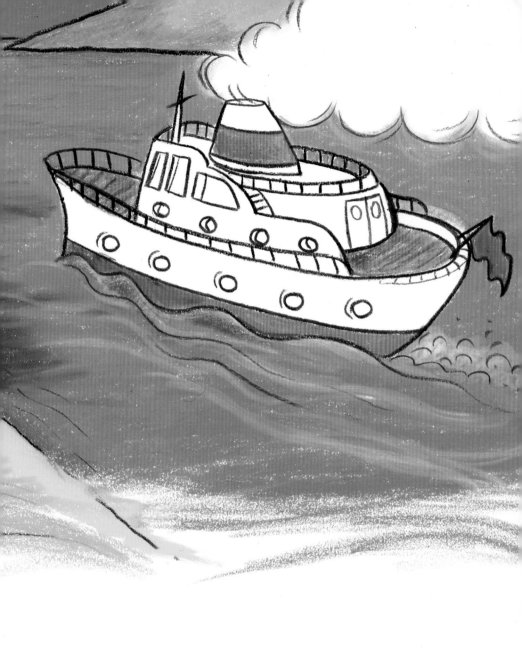

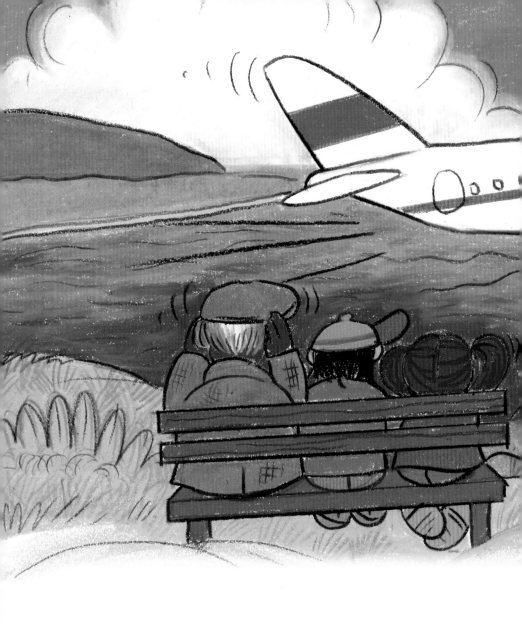

P is for plane.

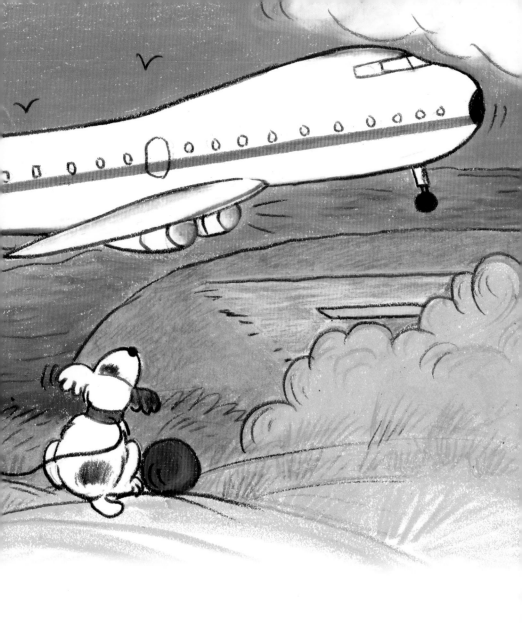

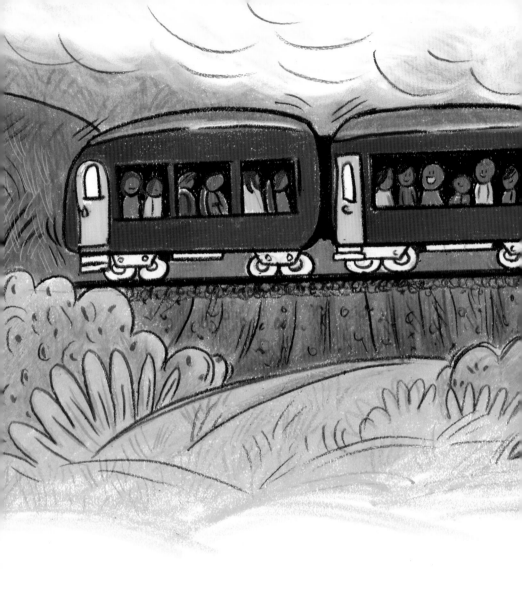

T is for train.

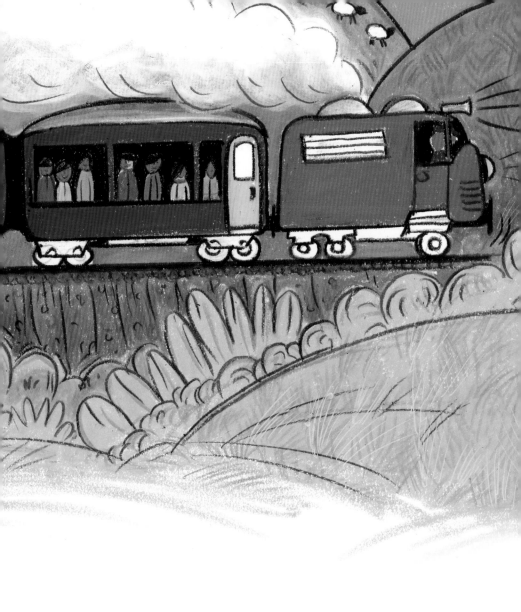

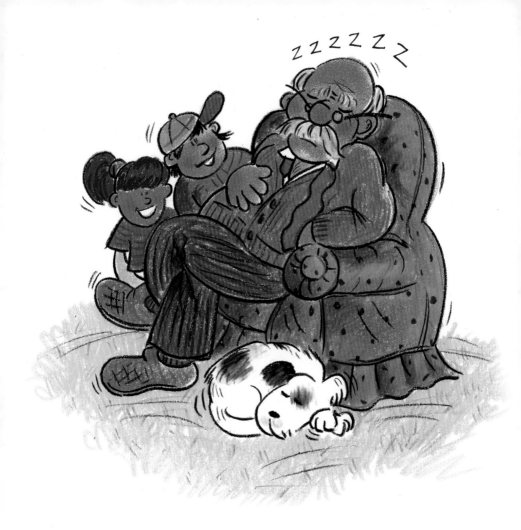

N is for noise.